SCARABEE, THE WITCH'S CAT

BY

MARY BLOUNT CHRISTIAN

ILLUSTRATED

BY

SYBIL McENTIRE

STECK-VAUGHN COMPANY

AN Intext PUBLISHER

AUSTIN, TEXAS

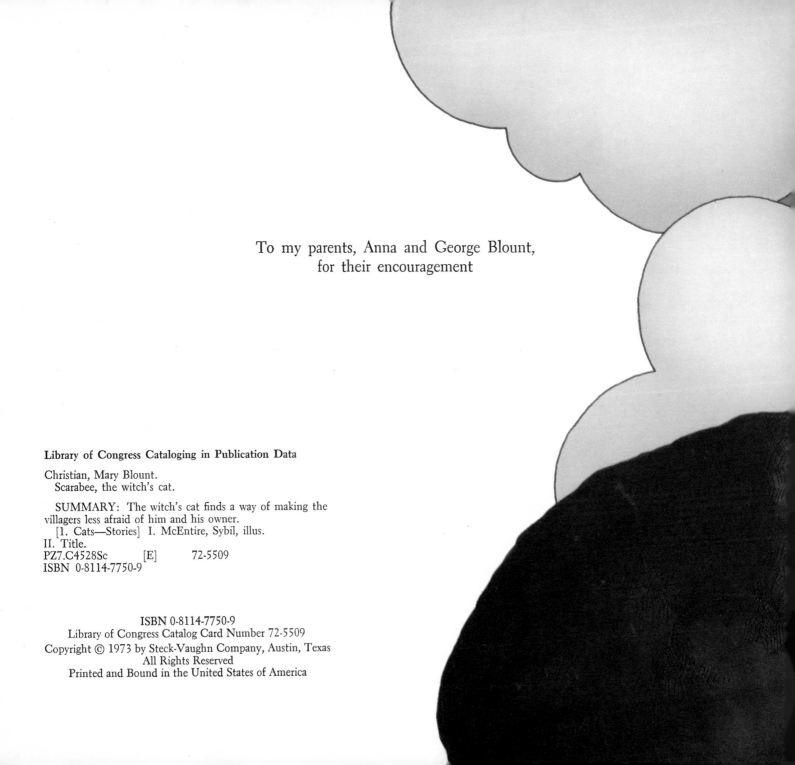

To my parents, Anna and George Blount,
for their encouragement

Library of Congress Cataloging in Publication Data

Christian, Mary Blount.
  Scarabee, the witch's cat.

  SUMMARY: The witch's cat finds a way of making the
villagers less afraid of him and his owner.
  [1. Cats—Stories] I. McEntire, Sybil, illus.
II. Title.
PZ7.C4528Sc   [E]   72-5509
ISBN 0-8114-7750-9

ISBN 0-8114-7750-9
Library of Congress Catalog Card Number 72-5509
Copyright © 1973 by Steck-Vaughn Company, Austin, Texas

In the tiny village of Samad-hi
a witch lived with her cat, Scarabee.

Each night, Scarabee sat silently
at the witch's feet as she stirred
her bubbly brews.

3

4

In the glow of the fire beneath the witch's caldron,
they listened for the laughter of happy children.
They listened for the chatter of happy villagers.
But the night was silent.

Black as a moonless night,
his eyes glowing like a jack-o-lantern,
Scarabee roamed the cobblestone streets
warmed by the morning sun.

5

Each day, he crouched in the shadows, his long, black tail silently switching from side to side.

Each day, he waited until a boy or a girl, a dog or a cat strayed near his secret place.

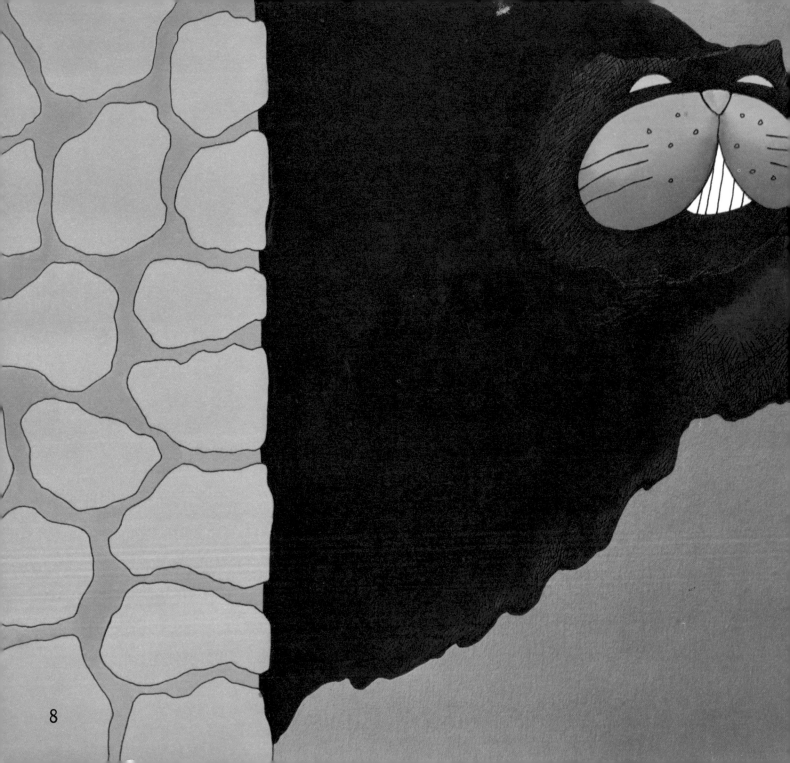

8

One day he happily sprang from the shadows.
His teeth glistened white in the sunlight.

"Run!" a boy shouted, hurling a stone
toward Scarabee.

"It's the witch's cat!" a girl cried.
"Run to your homes and lock the doors!"

9

The children scattered in all directions.
Scarabee was alone.

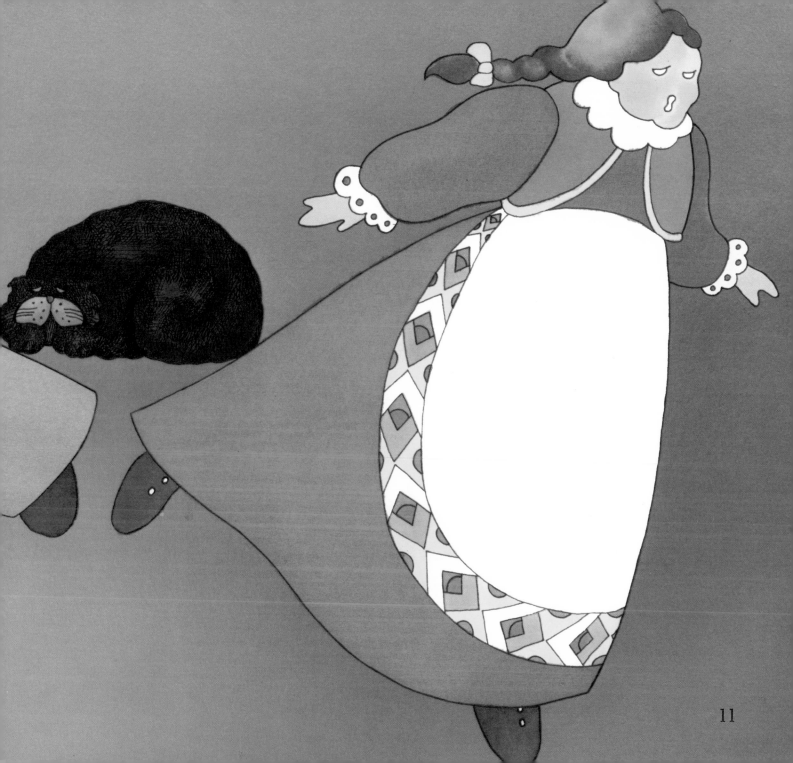

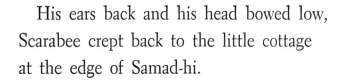

His ears back and his head bowed low,
Scarabee crept back to the little cottage
at the edge of Samad-hi.

There he lay at the feet of the witch,
watching as she bent over her caldron, stirring
and stirring a bubbly brew.

13

The two watched and waited. The brew bubbled
and boiled. But no one came to chat by the fire.
No one came to play with Scarabee. No one came
during the long, lonely night.

15

When the sun had risen, chasing the darkness into distant corners, Scarabee returned to his place in the village. But on this day he heard the sound of someone singing. He jumped to a window ledge.

Through the window, Scarabee saw a woman stirring something as she looked at a recipe. Something smelled delicious.

Children laughed and danced about the woman as she
playfully offered each a taste of her thick, brown brew.

When they left the room, Scarabee cautiously crept
inside. He stuck a pink tongue to the stirring spoon.
It was not like anything he had ever tasted.

19

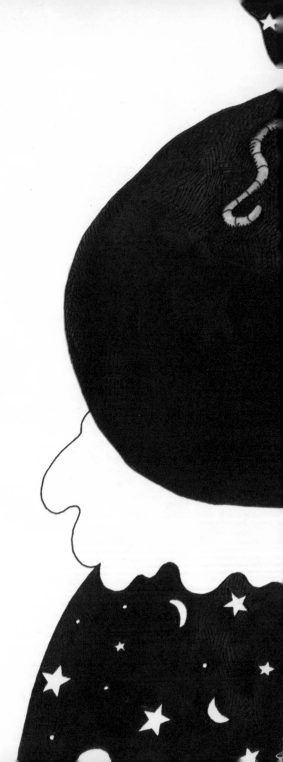

Carefully, Scarabee picked up the recipe
with his sharp, white teeth. He carried it
to the cottage and laid it at the feet of the witch.

Stroking Scarabee's fur, the witch read the recipe
over and over again.

"It must be new magic," she said. "Cocoa? Sugar?
Milk?" she exclaimed. "What strange ingredients.
Not a single bat wing or any cactus thorns!"

The witch poured the ingredients into her caldron.
Her nose twitched as she sniffed the sweet brew.

As the brew bubbled and thickened, Scarabee lifted
his nose into the air and breathed deeply.

The witch brought something from her pantry.
She put a pinch of this and a pinch of that
into the caldron. "There," she said. "These
will make the brew my very own."

THAT

THIS

23

A wonderful aroma began to drift from the cottage
toward the village of Samad-hi.

Children playing stopped to sniff the air.
Mothers sweeping floors stopped to sniff the air.
Fathers working in fields stopped to sniff the air.

One by one, they followed the delicious smell until
soon all of the villagers were at the door of the cottage.

25

But when the witch threw open her door, the villagers drew back frightened.

She smiled and waved her arm. "Come in, good people. Come in and share the magic recipe. Scarabee and I welcome you!"

Scarabee rubbed his shining fur against the legs of a village boy. He purred a loud welcome to all.

People were no longer afraid, and everyone went into the house. The children laughed and danced around the caldron. A ball of red yarn was tossed into the air. A mischievous boy tried out the witch's broom.

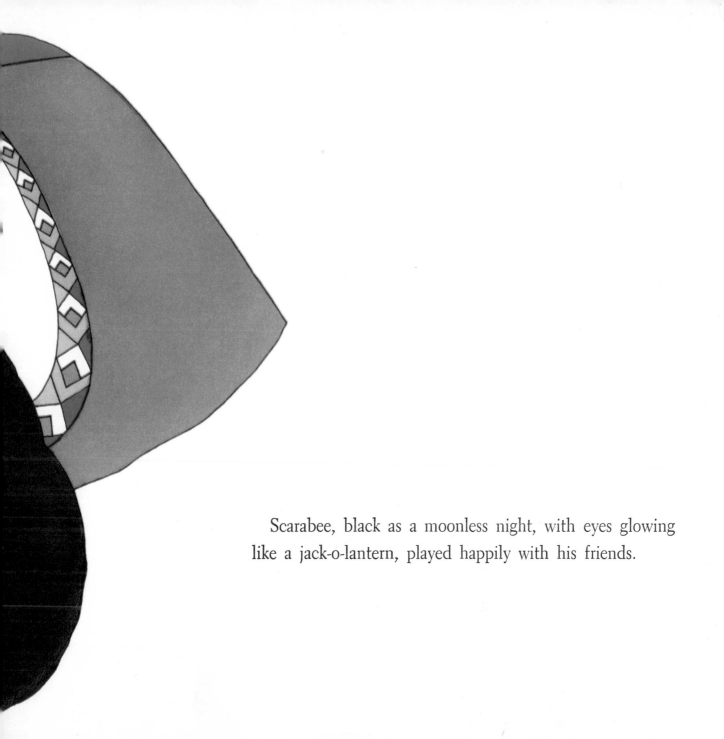

Scarabee, black as a moonless night, with eyes glowing like a jack-o-lantern, played happily with his friends.

And a smiling witch chattered with everyone as she stirred the magic recipe for delicious chocolate candy spiced with ginger, cinnamon, and mint!